BINDU CHELAT

12 unforgettable cab diaries of innocence, nostalgia and bonding

Of Heartbeats and Road Routes

First Published by

An Imprint of BlueRose Publishers

ISBN: 978-93-5668-603-8

Price: INR 150

Co-Author:

Editor:

Illustrator:

BLUEROSE PUBLISHERS
www.bluerosepublishers.com
info@bluerosepublishers.com
+91 8882 898 898

Dedication

To all who made my journey happen, for those who loved and lost in between and of course to those who remain!

Acknowledgements

My sincere gratitude to Benjamin Eric George who read all my cab entries without fail and selected the best ones, to Sunanda Chelat for editing without hesitation and to Rachel S Elizabeth for the illustrations that came from quick creative imagination.

A lot of regard to all Johnson IB Diploma students for their encouragement and for reading a few during the English class that gave me the push!

What makes it even better are the innumerable friends and well-wishers who wait to read whatever I write, even the small scraps and notes. You have always made my day.

Never having said thank you to my children Jo and Tan, here is one to them, to Joshua for being an indirect blessing and Tanya who is my lamp supporting every bit of this publication!

Foreword

The simplest experiences often teach us life's greatest lessons. Here is one such composition that will bring you to familiar roads – ones that you have stumbled upon incidentally, and others that you may have failed to notice amid the routine that pervades our daily lives. A brief pause, however, will bring to light several slices of life that instill within us a sense of revival be it through Baliah's moral residence, a family's trying recovery from the pandemic, or the humorous antics of a seemingly Americanised cabdriver. With the aid of her cab travels, the author finds solace in commoners' lifestyles and special moments that resonate in her mind long after their passing. Compiled from a range of over 100 diary notes, these 12 unforgettable entries truly encapsulate the essence of reality of innocence, of nostalgia, and of bonding. As the author travels through the underbellies of a vast network of city lanes and pathways, allow her to take you on this simple journey of life, love, and laughter!

Benjamin Eric George, University of Toronto

Illustrated by Rachel S Elizabeth

Contents

I heard life is hard
And it trapped me
I said life is easy
And I am liberated.
- Bindu Chelat

I love these little things, this cup in my bag with Professional Troublemaker written on it, this mask that can hide the silent smile and this song floating from the FM radio as I board the cab. It is a lovely day with little things in place.

The song is an old Telugu one and I am sure it translates like this: Life is…life is a holiday…throw all your worries away… (quite a welcome note).

The twinges of having had an argument with a cab driver who cancelled a booking is forgotten now.

The twinkle of having settled the score with him by raising a complaint too is forgotten. The song adds to the mood as FM magic continues blasting loudly and the vociferous RJ who is given his space in between the songs now announces names:

"Priya who wants customised jewellery for her wedding!

Praveen who wants to buy his dream car!

Padmini who wants to buy a dream flat!"

All of them appear lifelike and they can all get ready for their dream purchase!

"Advertisers can now declare their products as the prospective buyers seem ready…" the RJ continues.

30 seconds for all the propositions and immediately a soothing song follows probably about two butterflies who go out at noon.

The driver is also in a celebratory mood. We share a silent camaraderie broken suddenly by a sudden conversation on another end as he gets a call. But I am not too bothered by it. Maybe it is his next booking. No worries for me today. The next song continues about a willing sweetheart and a wooing lover conjuring to create a fantastic moonwalk!

I make myself more comfortable; throw away the grip of my laptop bag, push the lunch bag off and forget the cell phone. I want to reflect, reminisce, and wonder if life is really a holiday. But suddenly the car swerves and brushes past a truck.

The driver's conversation is ingrained with panic. The call is from his neighbour. I can very well follow the exchange of words. His father, a person with mental health issues, has left his room and has created a scene on the street outside his home. He consoles the neighbour without blaming his father. He promises to reach there fast. A son who is being put to test! Though calm outwardly the poor man is disturbed. It is his first ride of the day but not a very promising one. There is a moment of panic as he loses control and is about to bump into a bordering tree as I utter, "*Bhaiyya*???"

Immediately he collects himself and steadies the steering wheel. There is a teardrop rolling down his eyes as we now follow a garbage truck which has just taken over with the 'Keep Clean Together' logo.

The next is a Hindi song that begins "*Papa kehte hain bada naam karega*" (My dad says I will make him proud).

I alight from the cab, unable to help him in any way!

My heart aches though.

No one should be left without hope,
For even when everything seems fallen,
Hope lets you stand firm, move forward.
- Bindu Chelat

car cleaning hacks
CAB DIARIES
Rachel

I am hopeful today. I am hopeful that life will always grow me in all ways.

It is coincidental that the outer world too complements your inner thoughts sometimes.

I am ready to learn one more lesson, sometimes from trivial things and trivial patterns that go unnoticed.

Much to my happiness I get into a cab that is pristine from inside. It is definitely not a new car, but well-kept by the young driver who is brimming with enthusiasm and a smile unlike many others. His clean car portrays his personality. The exterior of the car is neat and free of dust, dirt, and grime. He gives a final touch up even as he waits for me. There are no traces of garbage, receipts, straw or wrappers in cup holders or door cubbies which are commonly left unchecked by some cab drivers these days. No trace of human odours or even a slight notion of human presence prior to my entry!

My finicky self when it comes to neatness in cars, compliments the young driver immediately, especially for the carpeting beneath the seats and the soothing fragrance lingering in the space. Rare are such niceties. The seat fabric and upholstery are not new but scrubbed to perfection. The dashboard sparkles and shines in the morning light. He seems pleased that I have noticed his hard work. With a broad grin of satisfaction he sets my destination on the device.

Probably sensing that I do not mind a conversation, he narrates to me some tips that he uses to maintain the cab.

"Shampoo is the best, madam, to clean the car exterior."

"Also, when you wipe the car do not do it in a radial direction, try to do it in a straight direction from one end to the other," the young man is enthused to delve into the details of the upholstery work.

"Madam, I had no money to do up the upholstery for this old car of mine, so I purchased towels and used them instead."

I take a closer look at the work. Seems impressive!

Though a university graduate, he is unable to land a suitable job. With limited options for his livelihood he has to run his old car as an Uber taxicab. The simple purchases of maroon towels and some green grass carpet sheets has transformed the interiors of his old car, now it has a clean aura. The small strips of green are really soothing to the feet. The maroon towels that are neatly spread add vibrance to the interiors. He has made the best of his limited resources. He seems to be making sustainable changes too by using DIY cleaners, space fresheners and bamboo reed diffusers showing travellers like me that all this is feasible.

He has given me a clean riding experience.

How enterprising!

Yes, it is true that there are things your money cannot buy!

Never deny yourself your true passion
To fit into someone else's dream.
- Bindu Chelat

student Loan → covid → Setbacks → Hang on

His Swag

You never fully know what you think you know darling for the people you meet and things they carry around themselves will sometimes break you free of your opinions!

Louis Vuitton, Gucci, Fiorucci and all their apparel advertising mannequins would have gone into hiding if they had seen my cab driver today. With a DIY pair of absolute rolled gold earrings and made to measure T-shirt, he carries a whiff of bespoke perfume. I also spot a large cherry blossom tattoo on his neck. His fingers keep tapping the dashboard as he hums a trendy English song alongside the stereo. A book lies beside the driver seat; I crane my neck to read the title: How to become a People Magnet. Oh yeah, I am face to face with a driver no more real than a rockstar, but with some subtle life hacks anyone can practice.

However, I am much bothered about the arrival time to my destination. Before the start, in my usual way, in Telugu, I direct him to take the right turn. But sharp came the whacky retort, in an immaculate American accent, "The left route is clear." Taken aback by an unexpected response, my nosey self does not refrain from questioning anymore. It is rare to meet fluent English speaking cab drivers, especially in this part of the town.

I ask him with restraint if he has been driving cabs for some time. He seems eager and willing to start a conversation. The story thus unfolds: incurring money on education loans he had gone to the US on a student visa, but Covid-19 derailed his life. Lack of compensation for international students, no stimulus help, no social help, no internship, no jobs to apply for, within a few weeks after the first wave hit the university authorities notified resident students staying on campus to leave, giving them less than 48 hours. Time and money lost to the pandemic. He has managed to drive his faraway cousin's cab to manage sustenance for some time but that too has its death knell.

"That moment in history will be defined not by what we had to deal with but how we dealt with it," he says looking at the horizon.

How plaintive yet how profound are his words: philosophy at the driving wheel!

Insurmountable setbacks at every turn in life has thus forced him to return to India. Back in the streets of his country, to me he seems acculturated and Americanised to the core.

Yet I find him poised to point because he tries...he also tries to retain his learnt accent, his style statements, his swag!

Surviving is easy

Surviving like another is hard

Though the road between you and me is equal

- Bindu Chelat

To the Statue of Equality

We are setting out today by cab to the see the statue of equality that embodies the tenets of the 11th century medieval saint Ramanuja Acharya. Maybe the master's folded hands will help me feel that my problems are not as big as they seem and maybe I will break free of my ideas about life and my potential and see the monument as a symbol of love. The related website alerts: A rallying cry, for people all over the world to come together in pursuit of a fairer, more compassionate place to live.

"All are equal in the eyes of God" how easy to say yet how difficult to practice dear Guru! My agitation is with the cab driver whom we have hired for this long trip to Muchintal, Ranga Reddy district.

The cab driver is rerouting continuously, yet from the car we catch sight of the golden gleaming statue afar. My nephew who keeps his travel journal handy as always has been reading up about the statue. He is quite astounded as we enter the vicinity of its precincts after several wrong roads but not having reached the car parking.

"Well Rome was not built in a day," he comments.

My friend wants to know more about the adage. Why Rome of all the places on earth? Why, for instance, when in Rome be a Roman? He quips further.

"Just be curious to know what is out there for you," says my son stopping the banter.

The cabbie has taken another turn. We can see the statue at a closer range, but we are just not reaching it.

The measured time has passed. We all become impatient, stiff, and brittle.

Several grumbling complaints emanate: Does he know the route well? Why is his google map giving wrong directions? Is this his first ride as a cab driver? How do all other cars reach except for ours?

But the cab driver who has roughened at surviving grumbling passengers keeps smiling. He tries to work out on the mistakes. He checks the route repeatedly and makes innumerable turns. We see the cars we have passed again and again! The grumbling only increases.

A turn here, a long stretch of road there, again a turn. After minutes of uneasy silence, there we are! The driver is unfazed. He keeps his cheer. As we alight, he looks at the blazing golden statue and says, "All roads lead to Rome".

He smiles in satisfaction, his smile reflected and refracted from Acharya's golden hue. I learn to laugh at myself though softly! I have not shown him the equality he deserves. He seems to know more than me!

The little girl said
People with money are not nice people
The big girl said
Money is relative to your behaviour towards it.
- Bindu Chelat

जीतें रहो • जीतें रहो • जीतें रहो • जीतें रहो • जीतें रहो • जीतें रहो • जीतें रहो • जीते रहो •

It is Monday morning and I too have my Monday blues. With anticipation of having a driver who can understand my broken Telugu, I pick up the call which the cab driver makes to confirm my location. Luckily, he speaks in Hindi. Though my idiolect is full of hiccups ranging from wrong words misplaced with the 'ee' and 'aa', he is quick to understand, and his voice seems cheerful.

I notice that my quirks and mistakes are soon forgiven as he tries to seat me comfortably. The camaraderie is a little confusing, but I don't want my wary nature to ruin the attention today. He starts the route map well on time though with a request.

"Madam can I stop for five minutes in the next lane to buy some breakfast?"

"Okay," I agree.

"I shall be very quick," he assures me as I look at the watch. I am 10 minutes ahead of time.

As he gets off the cab, I observe him running to one of the many breakfast carts arrayed beside the road. I wonder if he is picking up a package to eat later. But to my surprise he eats idlis in a hurry. As he gets a helping of chutney, he confirms my presence by glancing at me from that short distance. Poor fella…he seems so hungry. Hunger binds humanity. Hunger pangs remain the same for the prince and the pauper!

I utilize the time to make a few calls; he does make his way back soon. I notice his pickup order: a small package in his hand which he neatly places beside him.

Soon the cab swerves into the next curve and comes to a halt in front of a makeshift house by the sewers. An old woman wearing a gypsy skirt sits on a broken bench holding onto a long stick for support. She looks longingly into the distance. The cab driver slows down and hands her the package.

"See you tomorrow Maami," he says in Hindi.

"Jeete Raho," (May you live long) responds the old crone.

He relates to me that he had just 100 rupees when he went to bed. This ride that I took has given him a sense of assurance of some money in hand which confirms a breakfast, luxurious enough for a poor soul like him. But he does not forget to share his little joy with the old woman who once travelled with him on the same train as he came hunting for a job to the Southern part of India after the floods swept away his land and home in Uttarakhand. Though he seems unsure of his next meal, he remembers the elderly woman in his blessed moment and seeks her blessings through a simple gesture.

In fact, we all work for our daily bread…yet how much he gives who can so little make!

I alight into the open expanse of the yet empty parking lot with school buildings encasing education having learnt one lesson of mine.

27

This is not a comfort centre

But a growth centre

We are in Earth School.

- Bindu Chelat

CLASS II
ENGLISH
Date :
Day :
Aa Bb Cc

Things Begin at Baliah's Home

Today's cab driver is Balaiah, a man from Kakinada who does not feel it strange to grow up on watery soups or to wed a girl of his father's choice at 19. Traversing the traffic jammed roads cheerfully, he seems happy to have his cab taking its ups and downs merrily down the road. When job opportunities at his village shrunk, driving cabs in a city like Hyderabad seemed a heaven-sent opportunity.

Understanding my destination is the school, he starts talking about his school days. Days when teachers were respected. He does not seem to see that sense of respect these days. His recollections of his school days are about teachers who warned and punished him. If he brought complaints home, his mother insisted his teachers cane him more. Such was the respect commanded by the teacher. The cane and the teacher! The respect for the cane! The ironical respect for the caning teacher is all in place!

He seems disappointed by the grim realities of today. He has heard about teachers being threatened by students and parents for the simplest thing. His own children though are trained by him to be frightened of teachers, a sort of reverence that came with fear. He has seen to it that there is no word of disrespect from them. I believe in his sincerity. You know why? It's not because he has told me that his children read the Bhagavad Gita every day and avoid watching Bollywood films, it's because his wife and children have acclaimed him their hero. They show their love for him through simple gestures such as serving him water when he enters the house and waiting for him every night to have a family meal together. Where commonplace family meals have become rarities, I was happy to hear the last bit.

No wonder the respect for a teacher still holds in his family. After all, many things begin at home.

Yes! Live below your means
No, not by suffering
But just not the new cars, new house,
And then going somewhere quiet....
- Bindu Chelat

Covid Deaths
Hunger Deaths

Hunger Death Not Omicron

I walk quickly from home and down the tiled staircase to the road in front. I do not want to look around. Am I avoiding someone? I seem to be in such a haste. Outside the faint sunshine has a mysterious attendance in its glint, a cutting-edge glint as almsgiving to a chill December.

The driver is all covered in an old sweater, a shabby scarf, and a blue mask. His gaunt face is somehow veiled in brooding melancholy. As I seat myself and glance out the window, I still see the slight rustling of leaves drying themselves off the memory of rain. The driver wants me to verify my destination as there is some problem with the net connectivity today. I am aware that this happens frequently. A bad rain and there is a power cut. Networks get jammed and water logging is imminent. As though these trivial alterations would change my life!

In sombre stillness the driver is braving the roads, his steady gaze unwavering.

In a mellow voice he asks me if the students are attending school.

"A new variant omicron is supposedly out, Madam," his voice seems pleading, as though by saying the very words aloud would recreate a horrifying past.

One more lockdown is imminent, and I can see that it worries him. Already the working classes have suffered enough. The pandemic has sharpened the world's inequality. Hunger has been an immediate threat than the virus in many parts of the country.

Remembering some events during the lockdown, I ask him if the government has provided them free rations during the former lockdown. He tells me that rice and soaps had been given at first which were of good quality. With some forethought he scrounged up the little leftover money from meagre savings and purchased 80 kilos of rice promised at a lower price thinking that they must not die of starvation. He narrates that he comes from a joint family with many mouths to feed. But luck has not been too kind to them this time. He had to dump away the entire grains bought at a dear price as they were of very poor quality and inedible due to the odour that was released when cooked.

He relates that he does not dread the virus anymore but a lockdown that may cause hunger deaths at his home.

Ravi, Kamala, Pappu and the little baby! The old grandmother and his wife and her sister. I imagine them eagerly waiting for their next meal.

Nothing can save the poor if a corrupt hand is somewhere in the background. The country that has the largest food aid program just does not allow it to reach the needy. When civil society has lost humanity, what can be expected? I reach my destination but with a heavy heart. I will walk away and so will you. Won't you?

*****

Lean on relationships
Long walks and love lights
Replace screen time
With people time.
- Bindu Chelat

Will power, that weak yet inflated thing, hangs around my neck today morning as I enter the cab. Will power to gather energy and stamina to counter the day. Will power even to plan a trekking trip to Jim Corbett National Park. Will power to continue with the writing project about the Irula tribal girls. With impetus from above I am looking forward to a positive day.

Adding to the benevolence of a lovely day, this particular cab driver seems to have a personal commitment towards me. He calls me as soon as I book the cab and verifies the destination and the accuracy of my location. Of course, he has arrived on time and waits patiently. He even opens the door

for me. He is composed, confident and clean shaven. I have much respect for his space. We find ourselves setting out together towards our personal goals. The route is regular and once I am sure of it, I look out for the two trees I must not miss on my trip. A strange habit. Jacaranda and Flame of the Forest, I think so. At least I have given them those names. I pass them every day and I settle down in comfort only after I see them.

But a phone call from another end changes it all. Though the driver seems to put down the call twice, there are incessant messages from the other end. The loud beeps are embarrassing I suppose.

The fiery customer commitment I notice earlier gears into another direction. The furtive speech, the fluent rush of romantic dialectics, the varying promises of loyalty stirs fearful concern in me.

The mad distraction that is created by a sincere girlfriend on the other side must not put me in danger. Huge truckers are just making their exit. School buses are whizzing past. Many a swerve, many a turn is accosted carelessly as the conversation changes symphony and achieves crescendo. Pure oaths, hearts pledged for a lifetime, adoration and praise all merge at 7.30 a.m. I dab the droplets of sweat off my forehead and chant the name of God incessantly believing in the wonders of his holy name. Thanks be to God as love and promise meet. I reach the gate of my destination.

But my will power has cracked a bit. I feel sad.

Etiquette, commitment, focus, professionalism - words asserting identity are suddenly lost on the young driver as he makes conversation with a willing sweetheart. He has given me a jolt of fear today, yet I wish him well!

Maybe he will drive safe through the waters of love!

*****

You cannot weave dreams from threads of doubt.

- Bindu Chelat

Message under Duress

I will be offering my message under duress. A brave storm of words is under my lips. The judges who will be evaluating the students in this competition are from several other walks of life and I doubt their gauging abilities. Adding to the language distractions that hover across my mind as I recreate the vote of thanks, the rain too keeps smashing down on earth with unknown vendetta. It has wreaked havoc on its trail, leaving the route to work hazardous.

I wonder why on such days I am in such a suspicious mood. Rather than concentrating on ways to navigate to work, I am poking at boiled eggs at breakfast and fallen flowers; looking out for something to explode. I also suspect the excited voice of the driver to whom I am today's first ride. He has called me to confirm the ride. I don't see reason enough for his exuberance for life on a dull morning that seem to me a colourless leftover from yesterday's rain.

Moreover, news of suspicious cab and auto drivers are in circulation.

Daddy has proffered his extra information of theft in cabs around Kochi airport in Kerala.

Let me sit cautiously behind the driver today, cell phone ready and hands on the latch of the door.

Shared the trip details with my daughter already! Other days I don't bother.

She may pass on the information to her brother, and both would be tracking my safety. (High hopes, truth would be that she may not even notice)

Trust your intuition! My inner voice tells me; this man is seemingly happy on a lustreless day. He has a boisterous laugh that he has no right to. He applauds the boy in uniform who is carrying a flag to school. He shouts out his greeting to him. No bag but a flag! He can't suppress a giggle

100 for an emergency.

Pepper spray in the bag is old yet can do the work.

Dad's warning comes to mind: Never try to attack before the attacker counters you!

The opponent is always smarter!

Unfortunately, he takes all the wrong routes and then traverses back! He blames the Idea service provider connection smilingly; the routing is really bad.

"Change to Jio," I snap back.

"Idea is affordable," he mentions and continues unabashedly.

For each wrong turn, bigger the smile. I squirm, frown and fret. He senses my anger, but he smiles calmly and never loses his cool. On reaching school he jumps out of the cab and opens the door for me.

He retains his polite and smiling demeanour. I cannot help but let him keep the change.

Nothing compensates for his remarkable earth secret.

Is there a deterrent to save the destruction of a beautiful day with our ill-gotten temperaments?

My message to the judges will be delivered in grace. They have come this far without expectations. It will be one of gratitude, a gratitude that cannot be dwindled by doubts or distrust. I have my faith retrieved.

The sun shines after the rains.

People and systems count on our silence
To keep us where we are.
- Bindu Chelat

His Lord and Saami

Feudal order though not so visible yet runs deeply as an undercurrent within some communities and people here. I could sense before me the revered loyalty my cab driver posited for his boss who seems to me a feudal landlord at his native village. Little does he realise that he is being exploited. Even in a casual conversation with me he addresses him as his Saami (God) who provides him with his daily bread by leasing his old car to him during his crisis.

I have only asked him if the car belongs to him, and the story thus unfolds:

Having no access to education due to poverty or even the lack of aptitude, Ramulu lingered around as a decrepit lad in his village doing odd jobs for people. His mother who worked in his landlord's kitchen was thankful with the proposal of a car driver's work for her son who would otherwise roam around the village as a wastrel. Moreover, the threat of the youth being picked up by local police for unfounded thefts always frightened her. But the condition that was set before him was to keep 50 rupees at the end of the day and hand over the rest of the profit. The sum is meagre, but Hyderabad city has enough community kitchens and roadside eateries where one can manage somehow. He has thus arrived at the city to make a living for himself and his family. In the last one year he has been able to manage three more cars (the landlord's extending business) but for the same reward. He is happy as his mother has enough to eat at the landlord's kitchen. He does not mind the small reward as he feels he has something important to do. So much they have who so little give!

Human greed is disgusting.

What is wealth if it comes at the expense of others' lives?

A poor woman continuously works in a hot kitchen to keep her son 24/7 at the driving wheel in a hot city. Exploitation of the poor is a common phenomenon that resonates at the cost of dignity, autonomy, health and wealth, but it is rare to see someone succumb to its betrayal so naively.

As I alight and pay the fare, Ramulu continues to thank his stars and his Saami

If you're turning down jobs, you're not in a bad place

If you are crying about it, you are!

- Bindu Chelat

Anonymous Letter Writer

I am preoccupied today by the news of the anonymous letter writer who has been sending incessant warnings to school on the pretext of a student. Gossip has been doing its round for the past three days in spotting the culprit. Mischievous students who are shortlisted do not fit into the category. It is also bothering me badly, but I tend to remember reading Stacy Torres, assistant professor of sociology, University of California who states, "Gossip can stave off loneliness, facilitate bonding and closeness and serves as a form of entertainment."

Okay, so three cheers to such entertainment!

That special intimacy between fringe groups at my workplace points out to people who may otherwise go unnoticed. Even the watchman is not spared. Why would he write an anonymous letter though? Does he even know how to draft a letter?

Though such gossip drains me off my energy, I am also on the same page with others because sometimes gossip sounds better than truth.

Added to it all I find today's cabby very talkative and wants to know what I do at school.

For him schools do not denote just teachers and students. It is obvious from his question. For him it holds a sinister mystery I feel. I wonder what is on his mind. He wants to know about the admission fee, which is okay. Many drivers have asked me that question in the past. But then he wants to know the number of students. Then the strength in each class and student-teacher ratio.

Wow, that is some deeper understanding!

Volley of questions follows:

How many such schools under this same name?

What is the software we use?

Ah, the last question is quite absurd.

Maybe covid has given him enough reason to think, to evaluate.

But then a thought swishes past my mind.

But wait…Is he the anonymous letter writer?

By now he seems dubious enough adding to my scepticism, especially when my mind is off the cliff searching for the anonymous letter writer.

With his final question, I begin to observe him closely.

Rough, pragmatic, and no-nonsense standpoint; inability to feel joy for another's success or grief for another's defeat. One more reason for my doubt. Two cell phones, one iPad and a mini sound box on the dashboard. Wires around his ears. A Manila envelope on the nearby seat. And seems to be listening to my answers closely.

We get stopped at the main gate of the school. The sentry insists on him wearing the mask.

Aha…I laugh wickedly.

Would stop his incessant questioning now!

But he asks that one last question when he gets down: "Who checks your mail, Madam?"

"For what, why...?" I ask frantically.

"Want to apply for a job here as a school bus driver," he says abruptly.

In a grim tone he continues that he has heard about some school owners who have been paying full wages to all drivers during the entire Covid 19 period whilst others were getting laid off. He adds on that he has been bereft of cab bookings during the period.

I am ashamed of my doubts.

But the anonymous letter writer pops up sometimes.

Gossip does its rounds.

But it does keep away loneliness, creates stronger bonds and serves as entertainment.

The person who talks to you the most is you,

And birds and flowers maybe

You matter

Be kind to yourself and them...

- Bindu Chelat

It is a promising rain, a rain that will act as the umbilical cord to everything wonderful for earth hidden in its womb. But for me it looks like there will be no cabs available today. The roads are either waterlogged or broken with canals of water here and there.

Yet I have an unbelievable stroke of double luck this morning: A cab and a bird!

Word has probably been out on the bird wire about the high alert due to rains.

The Birdarazzi have been out in force in my little grilled corridor and some of them are already waiting there for more than three hours. The little sparrow is again there!

I have been thinking...Nah, not going to see him again. But here he is!

Here he is following me like a spirit from the past. A few metres ahead, and there he is posing and pecking nicely on the window. A little later he is flying low above my head swooping up and down and settling down on the railing as I take the staircase. Adamant about following me, he flits across the waiting cab and settles down by the bonnet in front. I should kick myself for not having bought a high-resolution camera yet. Here he is, seated well before me, also demonstrating nicely why he can be called birdie love or Lil birdie!

The driver is amused at my fascination. He does not start the cab, participating in the somnolent stillness as we both allow the little one his moment of farewell.

This little spirit from above, this little grey rainbow, this little promise of nature, the final survivor.

Maybe he will escape the harsh rain. Maybe I will see him again as I begin another ride. Maybe he will eventually find his way to the parks and forests where he belongs!

The driver understands how much I care for him. How sweet of him!

He does not want to crush the beauty of the moment.

He starts the cab only after he has flown away!

"And you? When will you begin that long journey into yourself?"

- Rumi

The best stories need not come from prodigious experiences, but from daily lives as we route through our turns, embracing the moment whilst capturing its essence, just like in Bindu Chelat's cab diaries titled "Of Heartbeats and Road Routes".

While the regular cab routine may just seem monotonous to everyday cab-goers, this author tried to make her trips museful by seeking for stories in her many trips assimilating her morning routine, nature's dynamism, changing auras, winding streets and most importantly the cabbie! De-route away from your regular day towards a destination of laughter, simplicity, emotions & tales of life as penned down not just from a writer's perspective, but that of a traveler, not across the globe, but through the very local streets between home & work. These 12 riveting cab notes, shortlisted from a 100 more, are sure to leave you smiling and pensive.

Tanya Sharon Francis

Bindu Chelat is a fervent educationist, voracious reader, natural writer and motivational speaker. She has taught English Literature for national & international curriculums alongside being a Principal, mentor and coach at prestigious schools. She embraces traveling & enjoys varied cultures and diversity. Her steadfast ardor for education and its power to positively impact the world remains at the crux of her undertakings.Words...oh beautiful words, the bridge between her and the boundless world! Unravel more of her persona as you read and connect with her works.

Printed by Libri Plureos GmbH in Hamburg, Germany